# Robert the Rose Horse

by Joan Heilbroner

Illustrated by P. D. Eastman

**BEGINNER BOOKS**

A DIVISION OF RANDOM HOUSE, INC.

To Peter and Barbara, with love
and
To Troop B of New York's Mounted Police

*This title was originally cataloged by the Library of Congress as follows:* Heilbroner, Joan. Robert, the rose horse. Illustrated by P. D. Eastman. New York, Beginner Books, 1962  64 p. illus. 24 cm. I. Title.  PZ7.H366Ro  62-9218  ISBN: 0-394-80025-7 (trade); 0-394-90025-1 (lib. bdg.)

Manufactured in the United States of America

Robert was a happy little horse.

He lived on a farm.

He lived with his mother
and father.

One day Robert had a party.

It was his birthday.

All his farm friends came

to the party.

They had a big cake.

"Happy birthday, Robert,"

said all of his friends.

"Happy birthday to you."

7

The cake was very pretty.

It had big red roses all around it.

Robert liked those red roses.

He put his nose right into one.

He took a big sniff.

Then Robert got a funny feeling.

His eyes began to itch.

His nose began to itch.

And then . . .

"KERCHOO!" Robert sneezed.

What a sneeze!

Up went his farm friends.

Up went the cake.

Up went the roses.

And Robert fell down flat.

His mother called the doctor.

The doctor looked at Robert.

"Say AH," said the doctor.

"AH," said Robert.

"AHA!" said the doctor.

"I know what made him sneeze."

"I know I am right," said the doctor.

"You will see.

Here, Robert.

Take a little sniff."

Robert put his nose

into those roses.

He took a little sniff.

Again his nose began to itch.

Again his eyes began to itch.

"KERCHOO!" went Robert.

BANG went the window.

BANG went the door.

Up went the roses.

And the doctor fell down flat.

"I was right," said the doctor.
"Roses are very bad for you.
There are too many roses
on this farm.
You must get away from them.
You must go to the city."

So Robert had to go.

"Good-by," he said

to his mother and father.

"I will be all right in the city.

I will find work. I will find a job."

Robert did find a job in the city.

He went to work for a milk man.

He took the milk man and his wagon
all around the city.

It was a good job.

And Robert was happy.

Robert liked this kind of job.

Then one day a man walked
right next to Robert.
The man had a flower in his coat.
The flower in his coat was a rose.

A rose!

And right under his nose!

Robert got that funny feeling again.

His nose began to itch.

And his eyes began to itch.

And . . .

"KERCHOO!" went Robert.

CRASH went the wagon.

SPLASH went the milk.

Up went the milk man.

And the man with the rose

fell down flat.

"Go away!" the milk man told Robert.

"You can not work for me any more."

KERCHOO

So Robert began to look for work again.
But it was hard for a horse
to find a job.
He looked for many days.

One day he saw some horses.

They had people on them.

"Say! I could do work like that,"

said Robert.

"I will ask for a job."

Robert went to the door.

A man came out.

"You look like a good horse,"

the man told Robert.

"You can work for me.

But you will have to work hard.

You will have to do

everything you are told."

So Robert went to work.

He did just as he was told.

When he was told to go slow,

he went slow.

When he was told to go fast,

he went fast.

Robert did everything he was told.

"I like this work," Robert said.

"And I am going to keep this job."

Then one day

he took a woman for a ride.

Everything was going well.

But all at once . . .

"Look!" the woman said.

"Look at those pretty roses.

I want those roses.

Robert, take me over there at once."

What could Robert do?

He had to do as he was told.

He took the woman

to the roses.

Again, he got that
funny feeling.
His nose began to itch.
His eyes began to itch.

And . . .

"KERCHOO!" went Robert.

Away went the wagon.

Away went the flowers.

Up went the woman.

And the flower man

fell down flat.

Once more Robert

was out of a job.

Robert had to look for work again.

He looked and looked.

Fathers had work.

Mothers had work.

Every one had some kind of work.

But there were not many
jobs for a horse.

Robert walked and walked.

He looked and looked.

Then at last

Robert saw something.

He saw a job he could do!

He could be

a police horse!

"I will go in.

I will ask for the job,"

he said.

When Robert came out

he was a police horse.

He was a good police horse.

He did all kinds of police work.

One day Robert worked on Bank Street.

Some men came down the street.

Three men!

One of them had a black bag.

They went into the bank.

Robert did not see them.

Then all at once . . .

Some one called out:

"Help! Police! Help!"

48

Robert looked around.

He saw the three men.

They were robbers!

Bank robbers!

The robbers ran right at Robert.

They ran right over him.

And away they went.

Robert got up fast!

He had to stop those robbers!

But how?

How could he do it?

And then . . .

Robert saw a rose!

It was not a big rose.

But it was a rose!

Robert began to think.

He began to think fast.

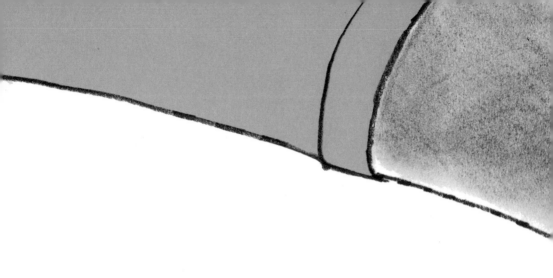

Robert went over to that rose.

He put his nose

right in that rose!

He took a sniff.

A big, big sniff!

And he began to get that

old funny feeling.

His eyes began to itch.

His nose began to itch.

THEN . . .

Robert sneezed.

Never was there a sneeze

like it!

Away went cats.

Away went hats.

Up went dogs.

Down came birds.

BANG went the guns.

Up went the black bag.

And the robbers fell

down flat.

"Hooray! Hooray for Robert!"

every one yelled.

The bank man was happy.

The policemen were happy.

Every one was happy.

Robert had stopped the robbers!

He had sneezed the robbers flat!

The next day there was a party.

It was for Robert.

His mother and father came.

His farm friends came.

The doctor came.

All the policemen came, too.

Then one of them got up.

"Robert," he said, "I have

something for you."

"ROSES!" yelled the doctor.

"Hold on to your hats.

Here comes a sneeze!

Robert will sneeze us all to Chicago!"

63

Robert took a little sniff.

His nose did NOT itch.

His eyes did NOT itch.

Then Robert took a big, big sniff.

He did NOT get that funny feeling.

That big Kerchoo had done it.

Robert at last was all sneezed out.

And roses never made Robert sneeze again.